Daisy Dreamer and the Totally True Imaginary Friend

For my family and fellow
adventurers of the imagination
—G. S.

Daisy Dreamer

and the
Totally True Imaginary Friend

#1

By Holly Anna • Illustrated by Genevieve Santos

LITTLE SIMON

New York   London   Toronto   Sydney   New Delhi

LITTLE SIMON

An imprint of Simon & Schuster Children's Publishing Division
1230 Avenue of the Americas, New York, New York 10020
First Little Simon paperback edition April 2017
Copyright © 2017 by Simon & Schuster, Inc.
Also available in a Little Simon hardcover edition.
All rights reserved, including the right of reproduction in whole or in part in any form.
LITTLE SIMON is a registered trademark of Simon & Schuster, Inc., and associated colophon is a trademark of Simon & Schuster, Inc. For information about special discounts for bulk purchases, please contact Simon & Schuster Special Sales at 1-866-506-1949 or business@simonandschuster.com. The Simon & Schuster Speakers Bureau can bring authors to your live event. For more information or to book an event contact the Simon & Schuster Speakers Bureau at 1-866-248-3049 or visit our website at www.simonspeakers.com.
Designed by Laura Roode
Manufactured in the United States of America 0217 MTN
2 4 6 8 10 9 7 5 3 1
Library of Congress Cataloging-in-Publication Data
Names: Anna, Holly, author. | Santos, Genevieve, illustrator.
Title: Daisy Dreamer and the totally true imaginary friend / by Holly Anna ; illustrated by Genevieve Santos.
Description: First Little Simon paperback edition. | New York : Little Simon, 2017.
Series: Daisy Dreamer ; 1 | Summary: "In the first book of the Daisy Dreamer series, seven-year-old Daisy Dreamer learns that everything she's ever imagined or drawn is all real! She meets her totally true imaginary friend, Posey, who invites Daisy to explore the extraordinary world filled with all the things she's always daydreamed about"—Provided by publisher.
Identifiers: LCCN 2016011902 | ISBN 9781481486316 (hc) | ISBN 9781481486309 (pbk) | ISBN 9781481486323 (eBook)
Subjects: | CYAC: Imagination—Fiction. | Imaginary playmates—Fiction.
BISAC: JUVENILE FICTION / Readers / Chapter Books. | JUVENILE FICTION / Imagination & Play. | JUVENILE FICTION / Fantasy & Magic.
Classification: LCC PZ7.1.A568 Dai 2017 | DDC [Fic]—dc23
LC record available at https://lccn.loc.gov/2016011902

CONTENTS

Chapter 1: Good Morning, Daisy!   1

Chapter 2: Upsy's Special Journal   19

Chapter 3: Morning Meeting!   33

Chapter 4: The Secret Journal Club   43

Chapter 5: Disaster Strikes   59

Chapter 6: Missing!   67

Chapter 7: Things Get Weird   75

Chapter 8: So. Totally. Cool.   85

Chapter 9: An Imaginary Friend   95

Chapter 10: A Whole New World   105

Good Morning, Daisy!

"Knock, knock!"

"Who's there?"

"Mom."

"Mom who?"

"Mom who's about to come get you out of bed if you don't wake up, Daisy Dreamer!"

"Five more minutes to finish my dream!" I say, like I do every morning.

Then I close my eyes and try to remember my dream, but *POOF!* Just like that, it's gone. I ask my pillow if it remembers. But it doesn't.

Aw, man! It was a good one too. . . . At least, I think it was. I sigh and flop over onto my stomach. Then I feel something tickle my toes.

"Daddy, *STOP*!" I shout as I squirm this way and that. "I asked for five more minutes! That was only *two*!" And I know I'm right.

Daddy laughs and says, "Wake up, Daisy Dreamer! You have to get out of bed, or you'll dream the day away!"

So I tug my blanket right off the bed and hop onto the floor. Then I zoom out the door, dragging my blanket behind me.

"If I can't stay in bed, then I'll bring my bed with me!" I hide under my blanket and walk slowly down the hall. My blanket is actually a magical robe that makes me invisible. Now I can sleep and no one will see me.

Uh-oh! Sir Pounce has found me! Sir Pounce is a cat detective and secret

spy for the United Pet Spy Agency. He has X-ray vision and can see through my invisible robe. He pounces, and *OWIE!* His claws are *sharp*!

"Okay, okay!" I say to him. "I'm *up*! And do you know what else? I'm *starving*!"

With my blanket still around me, I bumble down the stairs to the kitchen. My arms are stretched out like a zombie.

"Beware of the blanket monster!" I call out. I hear Sir Pounce race right by me. "Scaredy-cat!" I say and giggle.

As I enter the kitchen I drape my blanket around my shoulders. My blanket has now become a fur-lined cape. I am a princess for breakfast! And the princess would like milk and cereal. I shake some Toasty Squares into a bowl. Sir Pounce, my royal subject, gets kitty treats.

Then Daddy and I read the news. Daddy reads a big newspaper called the *Daily News*. I read the *Dreamer Report*, which is my very own special newspaper written by—ta-da—me. This paper has all the important news in the house. *Obviously.*

"Dad!" I shout as I wave the *Dreamer Report* in the air. "Did you hear there was a blanket monster sighting on the stairs this morning? They say it was *terrifying*!"

"Oh my!" Dad says, raising an eye-brow. "We'd better look into that right away!"

Mom sits and nods in agreement.

"Have no fear, Detective Daisy has it under control," I tell everyone at the table. "I'll get to the bottom of this blanket mystery, even if I have to go *undercovers*."

That gets a great laugh from my parents. This is shaping up to be a good day after all!

After breakfast, I cross my arms and become a genie.

"I wish my breakfast dishes would be clean!" I command. Mom says it doesn't work that way, so I clean the dishes myself.

Then I fold my arms, squeeze my

eyes shut, and make another wish. This time I wish for a peanut butter and jelly sandwich. And *guess what?* This time my wish really *works!* When I open my eyes, Mom hands me a peanut butter and jelly sandwich.

"I love magic!" I say as I plop the sandwich into my lunch box. Then I fly my magic carpet back upstairs to get ready for school.

Sir Pounce helps me pick out what to wear. He is my very own personal fashion stylist. Today he chooses a striped blue shirt with pink leggings and the perfect jean jacket. Cats make the best fashionistas! *Obviously.*

Then I brush my teeth and gargle my mouth-wash really, *really* loudly. Sir Pounce thinks I am a lion and runs away. Guess I'll have to fix my hair all by myself. I wear pigtails to tame my mane! *Obviously. Oink! Oink!*

I do a quick, quirky pose in front of my mirror. Look at that girl with black hair, freckles, and a button nose. That's me! Little do I know that I'm looking at a girl who is about to have the weirdest time of her entire life.

Upsy's Special Journal

But hold on, my day hasn't gotten weird—*yet*. First I have to run down the checklist that hangs on the back of my door.

Wake up. *Check!*

Eat breakfast. *Check!*

Find Sir Pounce's super-secret spy headquarters. Hmmm . . . maybe I'll have to find that tomorrow. *Skip for now!*

Pack lunch. . . . Brush teeth. . . . Fix hair! *Check! Check! Check!*

Wait! I almost forgot the most important thing! I grab my brand-new journal from my desk. I got it from Upsy. Upsy is my grandma, and she's the coolest person in the whole wide world. I nicknamed her Upsy when I was little because we totally belong together, like Upsy-Daisy. And guess what? She likes to write stories—just

like me. Upsy has the best imagination, too. Mom says that's where I get mine from, but I'm pretty sure it just comes from inside my head. Silly Mom!

Anyway . . . Upsy always tells me stories when she comes to visit. One time she told me about a haunted bowl of porridge. No one dared to eat it until a brave girl named Goldilocks tried it. Or the one about a boy named

Peter who could never grow up—that's because he was born floating five feet above the ground, and instead of growing up, his feet grew *down!*

I always beg Upsy for more stories. And she always tells me another. Then,

on her last visit, she gave me my very own journal. It has orange and yellow daisies all over it and a lime-green button with a pink satin ribbon around it. To open it, I have to untwirl the ribbon.

Upsy says this journal is for *my* stories. But to get me started, she wrote the first sentence of a story on special pages. Now I get to finish each one! And guess what she wrote in sparkly ink on the inside of my book?

Never stop dreaming.

That's a promise I *know* I can keep! In fact, I want to write something right this second, but . . .

"*DAISY!* What's taking you so long up there? It's time to leave for school!"

Oopsy-daisy, gotta go! I stuff my journal in my backpack, grab my skateboard and helmet, and then hop down the stairs like a frog. *Boing! Boing! Boing!*

Mom swirls on her scarf, and we leave for school.

Guess what? My mom and I go to the same school—only she's a teacher. My mom teaches the older kids in

fifth grade. We go to school together every day. Mom walks—*boring*. And I cruise on my skateboard—*fun!*

"What are you looking forward to at school today, Daisy?" she asks me on the way.

"*CHOICE TIME!!!*" I shout. *Obviously.*
Choice Time is when we get to do
whatever we want. "And I know what
I'm going to do today. . . ."

Mom grins. "Are you going to write
in your new journal?" she guesses.

I bob my head up and down as I clickety-click over the lines in the side-walk. I count the cracks all the way to Weaverley Elementary.

Mom gives me a great big squeeze when we get there. Then I step on the end of my skateboard and grab it with my hand.

"Dream big things today!" Mom calls.

I wave and run up the stairs to school. "Don't worry, Momma. I always do!"

Morning Meeting!

I'm in Mr. Roberts's class—room 2R. He is calling attendance while he balances a pencil on the end of his nose. Today he is being a seal. Yesterday he was a penguin. I love my class!

"Daisy Dreamer?" he calls.

"*AARRP, AARRP!*" I shout and flubber from my table like a seal to the Morning Meeting rug.

He goes down his list, calling out everyone's names. They all shout back and flubber like seals too.

"Lily Flores?"

"*AARRP! AARRP!*"

"Jasmine Wood?"

"*AARRP! AAAARRRP!*"

Jasmine is always the loudest. She doesn't sit at my table, and neither does Lily, but they are my best friends. We've always been best

friends because we all have flower names. And also because we've lived in the same neighborhood since, like, *forever.*

"Gabby Gaburp?"

"*BLAAH! BLAAH!* Whatever," she says.

Gabby does not flubber like a seal from her seat. When she

walks, she looks like a prancing poodle. Her strawberry-blond ponytail, which sticks out of the side of her head, bounces up and down as she goes. Gabby and I are not friends.

"Well, that *seals* it, we AARRP here!" says Mr. Roberts. "And you know what that means. . . ."

"*MORNING MEETING!*" we all shout. Everyone except Gabby. *Obviously.*

Morning Meeting is when we all get to sit together on the rug. It's my second-favorite time of the day because I get to

sit with Jasmine and Lily. *Obviously.*

"Okay, class. You know what's next. It's time for the Morning Mental Riddle!" says Mr. Roberts. We always have one.

"What building has the most stories?" he asks.

"That's easy. The Empire State Building," Gabby says, without even raising her hand.

"No, but good guess," says Mr. Roberts.

Everyone takes turns guessing—the Pyramids, the Eiffel Tower, the Statue of Liberty—but none of them are right.

Then suddenly I know, and I hold up my hand so high I could touch the sky!

"The library?!" I guess. "Because it's filled with stories in books!"

Mr. Roberts claps his hands. "That's right, Daisy!"

Jasmine and Lily cheer for me. Gabby crosses her arms and rolls her eyes.

"That's not fair!" Gabby complains. "She probably cheated!"

My cheeks burn. "I did *not* cheat!" I say. Mr. Roberts smooths things over when he says it is time to start the next lesson, which means we have to go back to our tables.

Unfortunately, that idea doesn't always work because I have to sit at the same table as Gabby. Ugh.

It's going to be a long day.

The Secret Journal Club

At recess, Lily, Jasmine, and I go to the Hideout.

The Hideout is our top secret space underneath the slides at the playground. There are no doors, and you have to crawl through a tube to get there. We've made it our own special place.

Jasmine's fountain of curly black

ringlets dusts the top of the tube as we go. She has to fix her purple headband after she climbs out. I cannot wait to show Lily and Jasmine my new journal.

"This is a humongous secret, *okay?*" I whisper as I carefully untwirl the ribbon from around the button closure.

Lily and Jasmine nod in agreement.

"We won't tell anyone," Jasmine whispers.

"Not a soul," adds Lily as she tucks a lock of her long brown hair behind her ear.

"We are now the Secret Journal Club," I whisper.

We quickly link our pinkies for a pinkie-swear promise.

Then I tell them how Upsy has written the beginning of a story on special pages and now it's my job to finish all the stories in the book. "And I want you to help me," I whisper.

"How do we pick which story to start first?" asks Lily.

Jasmine raises her hand as if we're in class. I call on her.

"What if we just let the journal decide?" Jasmine suggests. "Let it open to whatever page it wants. That way it will be a surprise!"

"Great idea!" I say. Then I rest the spine of the book on my lap.

"Go ahead, Daisy!" says Lily eagerly.

So I let the journal fall open. I look at the words and start to read. . . .

Once upon a time, there was a magical friend named

✦ *POSEY* ✦

"Wait . . . a magical friend named *Posey*?" Jasmine asks. "Is a posey a type of flower?"

"The flower is spelled *P-O-S-Y*—you know, like a pocket full of posies," I tell her. "But maybe adding an *E* to it makes it special, like an imaginary friend?"

"I like that Posey has a flower name like us," Lily says.

"Flower power!" says Jasmine, flexing her arm muscles.

We all laugh.

"Okay, the story starts here," I say. "What happens next?"

Lily leans closer to me. "It's your new journal, Daisy. Why don't you write something first?"

"Thanks," I say. Then I pull my ladybug pencil out of my pocket. I stare at the page.

"I think I'll draw Posey first," I say. "That will help me know what to write." Lily and Jasmine watch closely as I draw. The pencil glides across the journal's page. It feels like I'm not drawing at all, but like I'm tracing a picture that's already there. I can hear my friends hold their breath as I continue doodling. Posey has a round body, with lots of bright stars because he has lots of bright ideas. Hmm, Posey is a he? I never would have guessed! The pencil keeps moving, as if I am actually pulling Posey's image up from the blank page, like a magician pulls a rabbit out of a hat! Posey needs a nosey and a perfect goofy smile. And antlers. *Obviously*.

Once upon a time, there was a magical friend named

POSEY

Finally, I hold up the journal to formally introduce Lily and Jasmine to our first story mascot. "Secret Journal Club, meet Posey."

That's when someone from inside the tube says, "*POSEY? What kind of stupid name is that?*"

I hug my journal close to me. All three of us look at the entrance to the Hideout. Guess who just broke into *our* top secret hideout? It's Gabby and her grumpy, pointy-looking friend Carol Rattinger.

Ugh!

☆ Chapter Five

Disaster Strikes

"Gimme!" Gabby cries. Then grabby Gabby storms in and tries to snatch the journal right out of my hands!

No way, I think, and I hold on tight. Then *sha-rrrip!* The page with my picture tears. Right. In. Two. And guess what? I see fireworks spark out of my book. . . . Or maybe I'm just *that* mad.

Everyone freezes like ice cubes.

"Ooooh!" I wail. "My journal! My beautiful picture!"

Then Gabby shoves the crumpled, torn page in front of me.

"Geez, I just wanted to see what you were writing," she says. "If you hadn't pulled the book away from me, it never would have ripped."

I snatch the page from Gabby's hand. I'm too mad to say anything else. *Obviously.*

"Just tape it back together," Gabby adds, like it's no big deal. Then Gabby and Carol do a matching hair flip and crawl back into the tunnel like squeaky little meany mice.

As soon as they leave, my friends each put an arm around me.

"Gabby is the *gabsolute WORST!*"

says Jasmine, squeezing my shoulder.

"That creepy Carol probably put her up to it," Lily adds.

I smooth out the crinkly torn paper.

"You probably *can* tape it back together, Daze," says Lily. "It should be an easy fix." Jasmine agrees, and I feel a teensy bit better.

Then the recess bell rings. I am about to close my journal when I do a double take at Posey on the page. Did my drawing just *move*? I blink and look again. Holy daydreams! I think my drawing just *waved* at me!

once upon a time, there was a magical friend named ☆ POSEY ☆

"Hey!" I shout. But my friends are already halfway through the tunnel.

"Hurry up!" Jasmine calls.

I tuck the ripped page into my journal and hurry after my friends.

That did NOT just happen, I tell myself on the way back to class. *That was absolutely, positively just my imagination.*

Right?

CHAPTER SIX

Missing!

I count the minutes until the bell rings. Then I zoom away from school on my skateboard. I'm so boiling mad that I could turn to steam.

Mom is already home because her class had a field trip. She sees the frown on my face and tilts her head. "Everything okay, sweetie?"

No, everything is NOT okay, I think.

But I don't want to talk about it right now. I just want to fix my poor torn picture. *Obviously.*

"Everything's fine!" I say as I dash toward my room.

Mom shakes her head and smiles.

I head upstairs and search my room for tape. Sir Pounce rubs against me.

"Did you hide it, Sir Pounce?" I ask.

"Mer-rrrow," he answers as he stretches down low.

You're right, silly cat! It's on the floor under my desk! I grab the tape and open my journal to the torn page.

That's weird, I think. The piece of paper with Posey is MISSING! I shake my journal to see if it got stuck between the other pages. Nope.

I put on my thinking cap. Detective Daisy is on the case!

I dig through my backpack. I unzip my lunch box. I search all my pockets. Twice. I even look in my socks—because

you never know. But that missing page must not want to be found! How will I ever see Posey again?

"I can't stand that Gabby!" I secret-shout to myself.

Then I slump into a blob on the floor and blob down the stairs and blob into the den. I am blobbing toward the kitchen when Mom hands me the phone.

"Daisy, it's Upsy! She wants to talk to you."

I take a deep breath and tell Upsy about the terrible thing that happened. But you know what? She doesn't even feel sorry for me. She says, "Daisy Dreamer, I've learned that if the idea is good enough, it will always come back to you."

I sigh dramatically. Upsy is just trying to make me feel better. And guess what? She *does* make me feel a *little* better.

☆ Chapter Seven ☆

Things Get Weird

At school the next morning, we work on our Native American village project. That mean ol' Gabby acts like nothing happened.

She swishes her sideways ponytail at me and asks, "Can I have the glue stick now?"

So I hand over the glue stick.

Then she points to the purple

crayon next to me. "I need that purple crayon," she says.

I flick the crayon across the table.

"Hand me that ruler," she demands.

And this time I pretend not to hear and go back to work on my tepee.

As I draw a half-moon on the flap of my tepee I think about what Upsy said.

If the idea is good enough, it will always come back to you. But my drawing of Posey was not just an idea. It was an idea on a page—*a missing page*.

While I work, I try to wish my idea back. *Come back!* I think. *Come back! Come back!* But of course nothing comes back.

At recess, Jasmine, Lily, and I split
up to look for my torn page. We look
in the Hideout, around the swings,
and under the monkey bars. Nothing.
I head back to the blacktop. On the
way, something brushes against me.

I put my hand on the back
of my head. Whatever it is
falls to the ground.
Then I look at it
more closely.

"*MY MISSING
PAGE!*" I cry. And
I can't believe it, so
I bend over, pick
it up, and smooth
the crinkled page
out. But something's
wrong. Upsy's
words are still
there, but the picture

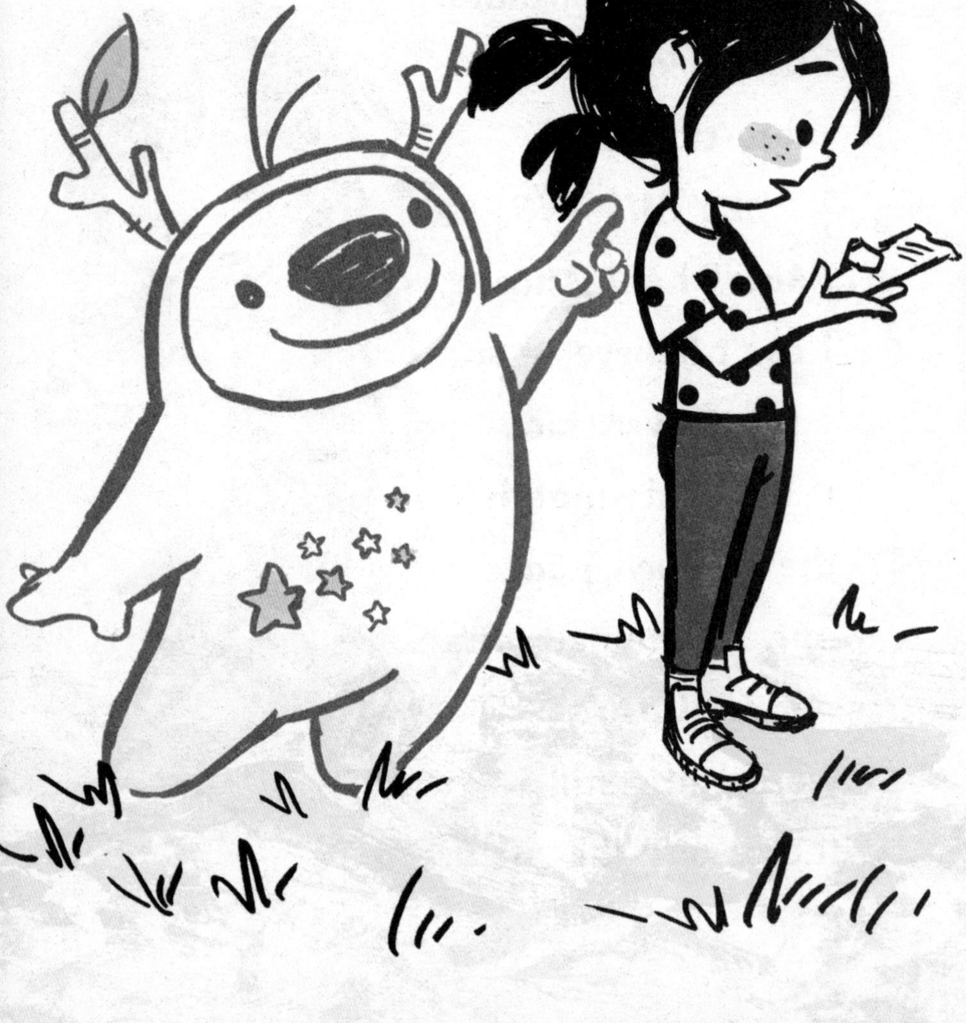

of Posey is *gone*! *Now, how can that be?* I wonder.

Then I feel a tap on my shoulder.

"Are you looking for me?" someone asks.

I turn around, and my eyes grow wide. *"POSEY!"* I cry, and I cup my hand over my mouth. My drawing is *standing* in front of me! And he's *alive* and *talking*.

Then I remember my manners. "My name is Daisy!" I say, and I hold out my hand. "Daisy Dreamer."

Posey stares at my hand and then back at me.

"It's polite to shake hands when you, uh, meet someone new," I add.

So he grabs my hand and shakes it—but instead of shaking it up and down, he shakes it *sideways*!

"Now you tell me your name," I say as the weird handshake continues.

And this question makes him laugh. "You know my name!" he says. "I'm *Posey*!"

And that's when things begin to get *really* interesting.

☆ Chapter Eight ☆

So. Totally. Cool.

"POSEY?" I cry. "But that's impossible! You're a DRAWING!"

He laughs even harder. "But I'm not *just* a drawing," he says. "I'm your *idea!*"

Then I pinch my arms, my legs, and my cheeks. *THIS IS SO. TOTALLY. COOL*, I think. Because it really is! I can't wait to tell Lily and Jasmine.

Then I glance around the playground, but I don't see them anywhere. I look back at Posey, who is staring into one of the classroom windows.

"Who's *that*?" he asks, pointing to himself in the window.

This time *I* laugh. "That's

you, silly!" I say. "That's your reflection." Then I wonder if this is the first time Posey has ever seen himself.

"Wow," he says. "I'm *magnificent!*"

And I blush because I'm the one who drew him! We're having so much fun staring at Posey's reflection that

I don't even notice Jasmine and Lily walk up.

"Daisy, what are you doing?" asks Jasmine.

Lily nods. "And who are you talking to?"

I whirl around. "Guys, you're not going to believe this!" I say. Then I point triumphantly at Posey.

The girls look to where I'm pointing. Then they look back at me and shake their

heads. I can tell they don't get it.

"It's *Posey!*" I cry. "He's *real!*"

Lily arches an eyebrow and looks at Jasmine. Jasmine looks at me and bites her lower lip.

"Do you feel okay?" Jasmine asks.

I raise my hands at Posey. "Can't you see him?" I ask.

They shake their heads again.

"Only *you* can see me," Posey says.

"But if you want your friends here to see me too, just say so."

"Yes, please!" I cry.

Then Posey snaps his fingers.

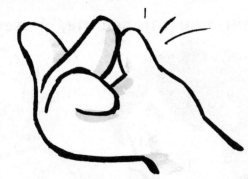

And that's when Jasmine and Lily gasp.

"Wow, he looks just like . . ."

"Your *drawing!*" says Lily, finishing Jasmine's sentence.

"Now do you believe me?" I say.

☆ Chapter Nine ☆

An Imaginary Friend

We pepper Posey with questions like:

"Where did you come from?"

"How old are you?"

"What's your favorite color?"

"Do you like ice cream?"

Then Posey spins around in a circle.

"I'm just plain old Posey!" he declares. "Daisy's imaginary friend."

We all shake our heads in wonder.

"Just think of me as a dream come true!" Posey says.

That's easy for me because Posey really *is* a dream come true. *My dream.*

And then, right in the middle of my happy thoughts, Gabby and Carol show up.

Carol nudges Gabby with her elbow. "Go ahead—show her!" Carol whispers, loud enough for us to hear. "Show her—I *dare* you."

Gabby has a piece of paper in her hand. Carol nudges her again.

"Okay, okay!" Gabby says.

Then Gabby shoves the paper in my face. "So, Daisy, we, um, found your missing drawing."

I take it and look at the picture. It's an ugly monster.

Gabby and Carol snort and giggle.

"And you know what's so funny?" Gabby adds. "Your picture looks exactly like *you!*"

Jasmine folds her arms. "What's the matter with you two?" she says angrily. "That's a rotten thing to say *and* a rotten thing to do."

Carol whips her black hair around and pulls Gabby by the arm. "Come on," Carol says. "That Daisy Dreamer

is nothing but a monster screamer!"

Then they walk off chanting, "HEY, EVERYONE! DAAAAAAISY DREAMER'S A MONSTER SCREAMER! DAAAAAAISY DREAMER'S A MONSTER SCREAMER!"

Right then Posey makes a magic move with his hands, and the monster picture I am holding zooms after Gabby and Carol. The ugly picture bounces in front of their faces, and both girls scream in surprise.

Jasmine, Lily, and I burst into laughter. Actually, the whole playground burst into laughter too!

Posey makes the paper dance and chase the girls all over as they try to escape. Up the slide, down the slide, and behind the swings, there's nowhere to hide from the monster they drew.

Hmm, I'm going to *LIKE* having an imaginary friend, I think with a smile.

☆ Chapter Ten

A Whole New World

"How was your day?" Mom asks. Mom always asks me about my day on the way home from school.

I whiz by her on my skateboard. Posey floats alongside me. Mom can't see him. *Obviously.*

"Today was only the best day of my *entire life!*" I answer. Then I look back over my shoulder to see Mom's face. She has on a really huge smile.

"That's great to hear, Daisy. What made it so special?" she calls after me.

"My imagination!" I shout.

Posey races next to me and sees a gray car pass by. He stops short. I veer away to avoid bumping into him.

"What's *that*?" he exclaims. "An elephant on wheels?"

I almost fall off my skateboard. "It's just a minivan," I say. "They're pretty common around here."

Hmm, I guess they don't have cars where Posey comes from. It seems like there are a lot of things they don't have where Posey comes from.

At home Posey gets into everything. Actually, he goes a little *bonkers*.

First he opens and closes all the kitchen cupboards. Then he pulls all the vegetables out of the refrigerator, and I have to put them all back. *Obviously*.

But Posey kicks a head of lettuce into Sir Pounce's cat dish. The kibble explodes *everywhere*.

Then Mom calls from her office, "What's going on in there?"

"Stepped on the cat dish!" I say, and I quickly sweep up the kibble and put back the veggies.

Sir Pounce comes to check on his dish. That's when Posey decides to

introduce himself to my cat. He shakes Sir Pounce's paw. But Sir Pounce pulls it back and runs away.

"Oh no. We are not friends?" Posey questions.

I roll my eyes. "Sir Pounce is a spy," I say. "Spies trust no one."

Posey nods and walks into the

bathroom. This time he introduces himself to the *toilet*. He grabs the handle and shakes it up and down. The toilet flushes and gurgles. Posey watches the water swirl in the bowl. Then he flushes it again and again.

And now he is very good friends with the toilet.

Next I steer Posey upstairs. He notices a light switch in the hall and flicks the switch. The lights come on. He smiles. He flicks it again. The lights go off. Then *on*. Then *off*. *On-off. On-off. On-off . . .*

"Daisy, why are the lights flicker-
ing?" Mom calls again.

I hold the light switch in place.
"Just my pretend dance party, Mom!"
She doesn't ask any more questions.

Phew! Then I push Posey into my bedroom and shut the door. I run to my bathroom and shut that door too. No more toilet flushing! I hurry back into the room only to find Posey swinging from my ceiling fan!

"POSEY, STOP!" I shout.

Posey hops down.

I drop onto the bed. "You're such a mischief maker!" I say breathlessly.

He smiles. "I was just saying hello to everything," he says. "Your world is so new to me."

I look around the room and try to imagine it all being new. "Well, you don't need to introduce yourself to everything," I say. "Hmm, if you don't have cars, toilets, light switches, or ceiling fans in your world—what *do* you have?

Posey plunks down on the bed beside me. "Magical stuff," he says.

"Magical stuff?" I say, because if there's one thing

I like, it's magical stuff. "What kind of magical stuff?"

"Would you like to see for yourself?" he asks.

I think my eyes might just pop right out of my head. "Would I *ever!*"

Posey hops off my bed. "Then let's go!" he says.

"Just like *that*?" I question.

"Just like that," he says.

Oh wow, I think. *Is this really true? Is this really happening to me? Am I, Daisy Dreamer, actually going to visit an imaginary world . . . ?*

Check out Daisy Dreamer's next adventure!

Is this really true? Is this really happening to me? Am I, Daisy Dreamer, actually going to visit an imaginary world . . . ?

"Are you ready, Daisy?" asks Posey, my very real imaginary friend.

I think hard. But only for one

second, because do I want to see a world full of magical stuff? You better believe I do!

"YES!" I shout out and jump, jump, jump for joy. *Obviously*. "But how do we get there?"

Now, I have been to lots of places in my life. I've been to my grandma Upsy's house, and I went to the aquarium on our first-grade field trip. I've even had a sleepover at my best friend Lily's house! But I've never been someplace imaginary.

Posey doesn't answer my question. He's too busy going through my stuff.

Excerpt from *Daisy Dreamer and the World of Make-Believe*

So how do you get to an imaginary place? I ask myself. *Do you have to wear magic shoes? Or fly on a winged hippopotamus? Or take a hot-air balloon?* Then *WHACK!* A sock hits me in the side of the head.

"OW!" I say, even though it doesn't really hurt.

Then *WHOOSH!* I duck out of the way of my hairbrush just in time. *Hey, that WOULD have hurt!* I say to myself, and I shield my head with one hand.

"What do you think you're DOING?!" I shout as things continue to fly across my room.

Excerpt from *Daisy Dreamer and the World of Make-Believe*